The Mermaid
of Zennor

To Judy Floyd
C.C.

For my friend, Charles Causley
M.F.

ORCHARD BOOKS
338 Euston Road, London NW1 3BH
Orchard Books Australia
Level 17/207 Kent Street, Sydney, NSW 2000
ISBN 978 1 40831 954 3
First published in 1999 by Orchard Books as *The Merrymaid of Zennor*
First published in paperback in 2001
This edition published in 2012
Text © Estate of Charles Causley 1999
Illustrations © Michael Foreman 1999
The rights of Charles Causley to be identified as the author and Michael Foreman
to be identified as the illustrator of this work have been asserted by them in
accordance with the Copyright, Designs and Patents Act, 1988.
2 4 6 8 10 9 7 5 3
A CIP catalogue record for this book is available from the British Library.
Printed in China

Orchard Books is a division of Hachette Children's Books,
an Hachette UK company.
www.hachette.co.uk

The Mermaid of Zennor

Charles Causley

Illustrated by Michael Foreman

ORCHARD

ZENNOR lies beside the Cornish sea in West Penwith, the most mysterious part of all Cornwall. There are no trees. The land wears only a thin covering of earth. Scattered about are reminders of the folk who lived here thousands of years ago.

There are standing-stones, cromlechs and the huge boulders which were thought to have been used by the giants in their games. And everywhere, still, are the stone stacks of chimneys and engine-houses marking the presence of the mines.

There lived Zachy Pender, the farmer's son whose home was a mile or more from any neighbour, but this bothered him not at all. He was not a lonely boy. He simply enjoyed his own company and was never happier than when wandering the cliffs or the high moor and making up stories in his head about the people of long ago.

And Zachy was just as happy singing in the church choir of a Sunday. It was said in those days that the people of Zennor were the finest singers in Cornwall, and young Zachy was no exception. Nor was Zachy's friend Tom Taskis.

Tom Taskis was a tin-man. Six days out of seven he worked in the dark and wet and heat of the mine. He lived in a little granite cottage just half-way between Zachy's home and the church.

Every Sunday morning Zachy would call on Tom and together they walked to church to sing in the choir. They made a fine pair as they strolled along together, scrubbed and smart in their Sunday best. They didn't say much. But if Zachy had an older brother it's clear he'd have wished him to be like Tom. Likewise Tom with Zachy.

It was one sunny Sunday morning that Zachy first noticed the beautiful young woman sitting very straight in the single, carved oak chair at the very back of the church. Tom noticed her too.

She was a pretty girl and no mistake. Her hair, where it escaped from a bonnet shaped curiously like a shell, shone like a coil of gold. As for her gown, it was of a glimmering, silken silver that swirled about her like a wave of the sea.

Next Sunday, there she was again in her chosen place. Sunday after Sunday she reappeared, each time leaving as mysteriously as she had come. And each time they saw her, Zachy and Tom exchanged glances as if to say, 'Here she is again, then!' But, strangely, neither mentioned it to the other. Nor, it seemed, did they feel it necessary to do so.

On the seventh Sunday was the most remarkable happening of all. While the rest were busy singing the last hymn, Tom Taskis suddenly stepped out of his choir-stall and walked straight down the aisle to where the lovely girl was standing. He took her by the hand and together they disappeared through the great doorway.

Nobody seemed to notice them go. Nobody, that is, except Zachy Pender.

As soon as ever he could, Zachy was racing down the churchyard steps after them. He squizzed and squinted this way, that way.

Nothing. Nobody.

Then he spied the couple. At once he made after them, keeping well out of sight.

When Tom Taskis and the stranger reached the rushing Stream-with-no-Name that plunged from the high moor down to the sea, what did they do but leap, hand in hand, into its peaty water. As they did so, Tom Taskis caught Zachy's eye and placed a finger across his lips as if to say, 'Don't say a word, my friend! Not a word!' Then the stranger's glimmering robe fell away and Zachy saw that she sported not two human feet but a pair of gleaming fish's fins.

She was a merrymaid!

Zachy was so surprised and delighted that he could barely think. As for telling the rest of the village – well, now, who would believe such a tale from Zachy Pender, the maker of stories?

Almost a year drifted by. Curiously, nothing much was said in the village of the strange affair of Tom Taskis and his disappearance. Such things had happened before in Zennor. Without a word to others, young women and especially young men had left home to try their fortunes beyond Cornwall, and often beyond the sea.

At first, Zachy missed his friend. But as the weeks and months passed, it seemed almost as if he had forgotten the affair of Tom Taskis and the merrymaid.

It took an October gale, the fiercest along the coast for many years, to blow it back into his mind again.

Zachy lay in his bed marvelling at the sound of the winds and the waves. He thought of stories he had heard of fine sailing-ships that had taken refuge in the cove below Zennor to escape the anger of the sea. But Zachy had seen not a single one.

All at once he made up his mind. "It's now or never," he said.

Tugging on his trousers, he crept downstairs, hitched an oilskin over his shoulders and gently let himself out by way of the back door.

Night was turning into day. Zachy hurried through the village and made his way towards the cliff-top.

Would he see a sailing-ship? It was as if the sea itself answered his question.

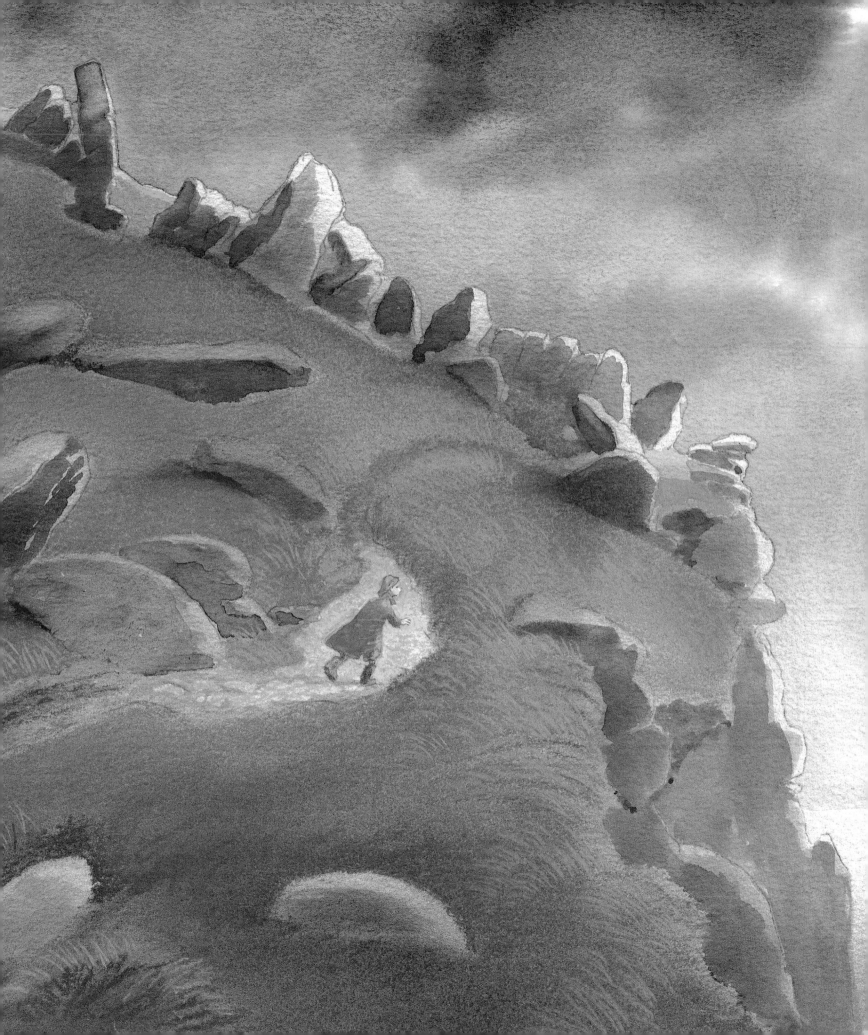

He heard, from far below Zennor Head, a great thrust of water burst from the famous blow-hole down there which, in stormy weather, swallows great gulps of the high sea only to spray them out again a hundred feet and more above the cliff-top.

The waters rose up in a huge curve over Zachy's head and fell to earth just beyond him, exploding in millions of watery fragments. Zachy threw up his arms to protect himself from the salt-sea drops that for a moment blinded him.

Then there was such a sound as he never had heard in his life before. It was the strangest small cry. A kind of keening or wailing.

Woo-hoo! Woo-hoo! Woo-hoo!

It had something of the low moan of a razorbill.

The tiny *grizzle* of a puffin.

The sorrowful *hoo-ee!* of a seal.

Very cautiously, Zachy opened one eye.

Then the other.

What do you think he saw?

Directly in front of him, safe on a soft bed of bracken and heather lay a baby.

It clenched and unclenched its fists and waved its arms wildly. But this was no earthly child. The lower half of its body was that of a fish. And instead of feet, a pair of shiny fins turned now this way, now that.

No doubt about it. This was a merrychild, and its mother must be a merrymaid.

It was the most beautiful creature Zachy had ever seen. It stared up at Zachy, plainly in terror for its life.

Zachy had no notion of whether or not the merrychild could understand him. But, "Don't worry, midear," he said in the kindest voice he could muster. "I'll soon see that you're safely back where you belong."

Seizing up the merrychild and holding it tight, Zachy turned and as fast as he could ran back the way that he had come. At last he reached the Stream-with-no-Name. As he made to follow its course down to the cove, he saw a second astonishing sight.

Swimming powerfully upstream was the lovely merrymaid of all those Sundays before. In its joy at the sight of the merrymaid, the little merrychild almost slipped from Zachy's hold.

With an amazing leap through the air, the merrymaid grasped the merrychild from Zachy's arms, turned about and re-entered the stream as it raced down to the cove. As she did so, she smiled at Zachy - a wonderful smile - and from a cluster of what looked like jewels about her throat she threw him a small, gleaming object. As it flew through the air it flashed in the morning light.

Zachy caught it easily. It was a curious little shell, the like of which he had never seen before. Its outside was of silver. The inside was of pure gold.

Again, Zachy told no-one of what had happened and what he had seen.

Soon it was summer again. Zachy, his back to the sea, was spearing thistles in his father's field above the cove.

He never could tell just what it was that made him suddenly spin round and look down at the ocean far below.

Lying in the bay was a handsome sailing-ship. Three seamen, and a fourth man, seemingly the Captain, were in the act of lowering the anchor. This done, they leaned over the ship's side and gazed down into the water. Quite without warning, a figure rose from the depths of the sea and broke the calm surface of the bay.

It was the merrymaid!

Her voice, pure as the note of a bell, floated up to where Zachy was
standing. "Captain!" she called. "Please, please raise the anchor! It is lodged
directly before the entrance to my secret sea-cave beneath the waters.
I cannot enter, and my dear children and husband are imprisoned within!"
Not wishing to harm or offend the creature, the Captain and his men
weighed anchor with all speed. As it was hauled dripping from the sea,
the merrymaid plunged out of sight. At that very moment a strong breeze
arose, filling the sails of the ship as it moved gracefully out of the cove.

Almost at once the merrymaid reappeared, smiling. At her side, also smiling, was a handsome, dark-haired young man. Zachy recognised him at once.

Tom Taskis.

A smaller figure came to the surface. Its golden hair glinted in the sun. It was the very same merrychild, now grown a little older, that Zachy had rescued on the night of the great storm.

Another merrychild appeared. And another. Seven in all.

By this time, the merrymaid and Tom Taskis had
spotted Zachy standing at the top of the cliff. Soon,
the merrychildren saw Zachy too.

Smiling, the merrymaid and Tom Taskis and
all the merrychildren swam in a merry circle,
waving joyfully to Zachy.

Then, as if at some signal, they all dived
out of sight and were seen no more.

Zachy shook his head in wonder. He took his tiny silver and gold shell from his pocket and gazed at it for a moment. "I know what I'll do," he said to himself as he walked slowly home. "When I am a grown man, I shall tell of all this to my dear wife and children so that the tale may be remembered for all time."

And so he did. Neither Tom Taskis, nor the beautiful merrymaid nor a single merrychild was ever seen again in Zennor. All that remain are the words of Zachy's story, and the oak chair with its carving of the strange sea-creature that still stands in the church as a reminder of when the merrymaid came up from the Zennor strand to walk upon the Cornish land.

About the village of Zennor

In Cornwall a mermaid is also known as a merrymaid. The coastal village of Zennor lies about four miles west of St Ives on the road to St Just and Land's End. If you visit Zennor's beautiful little parish church of St Senara you will find an ancient bench-end, now made into a heavy chair, on which is carved the figure of a merrymaid. She is combing her hair and has a comb in one hand and a looking-glass in the other.